This book belongs to:

St. Ninians Old Parish Church . . . .

Contents

Peppa Pig™

Fun at the Fair

Today, Peppa and her family are at the funfair.
"Snort! Slidey, slidey!" giggles George.
"George wants to go on the
helter-skelter," says Daddy Pig.
Daddy Pig and George head off to
the helter-skelter.

3

"Roll up! Roll up!" cries Miss Rabbit.
"Hook a duck and win a giant teddy!"
"I'll try to win one for you, Peppa," says
Mummy Pig. "But I don't think it's that easy!"
"It's impossible!" laughs Miss Rabbit.
"We'll see about that!" cries Mummy Pig.

Sploosh! Mummy Pig has hooked a duck!
"Hooray!" cheers Peppa.
"That's amazing!" cries Miss Rabbit.
"Here's your giant teddy!"
"Wouldn't you like a little teddy instead, Peppa?"
"No way!" giggles Peppa, happily.

George and Daddy Pig are at the helter-skelter.
"Hmm, it's a bit high, George. Are you sure you want to have a go?" asks Daddy Pig.
George giggles and runs up the stairs to the top.
It's a bit too high and George starts to cry.
"Don't worry, George. I'll come up with you," says Daddy Pig.

"Hee, hee! Weeeeeeee!" cries George,
sliding all the way down the helter-skelter.
Now, George is having too much fun to be scared.
"It is a bit high," says Daddy Pig nervously.
Daddy Pig is more scared than George.
Oops! Daddy Pig slips down the slide!

Wooahhh!

Peppa and Mummy Pig are at the
'Hit the Target' stall.

"You can do that easily, Mummy," says Peppa.
"Ho, ho! You won't win!" laughs Mr Labrador.
"Women are useless at this!"
"What did you say?" says Mummy Pig crossly.
She picks up the bow and arrow and aims . . .

Whoosh!
The arrow hits the target
right in the middle.

Mummy Pig wins again!

"Unbelievable," cries Mr Labrador. "Here's your teddy!"

"Hooray!" cheers Peppa.

Now she has two giant teddies.

Daddy Pig and George are
riding on the big wheel. George loves it,
but Daddy Pig is a little bit scared.
"This really is high!" says Daddy Pig, as the
big wheel goes round and round.
"Hee, hee! Snort!" giggles George.

Daddy Pig and George find Peppa and Mummy Pig.
"Hit this button with a hammer," says
Mr Bull. "If the bell rings, you win a prize!"
"I'll have a go," says Daddy Pig. "Stand back!"
"I think you're a bit wobbly from the big wheel!"
says Mummy Pig.

"Ho, ho!" laughs Mr Bull.
"Daddy Pig is looking a bit shaky!"

"What?" says Mummy Pig, crossly.
"Give . . . me . . . that . . . hammer!"
Whack! Mummy Pig hits the button
as hard as she can.
The bell rings loudly. Ding! Ding! Ding!

21

Everyone is very impressed. Mummy Pig wins
all the giant teddies at the fair!

"Hooray!" cheers Peppa and she gives all of
her friends one giant teddy bear each.
"Hooray!" everyone cheers. "We love funfairs!"

George's First Day at Playgroup

Today is George's first day at playgroup.
"Isn't George too small for playgroup?" asks Peppa.
"You can look after him," says Daddy Pig.
Peppa isn't sure she wants George at
her playgroup, but she likes the idea of
looking after him.

"Are you sure George is big enough?"
Peppa asks when they arrive.
"Yes, he'll be fine," replies Daddy Pig.
"OK. He can come," says Peppa.
She holds onto George's hand.
"Grunt! Grunt!" snorts George, jumping
up and down.

Here is Madame Gazelle, Peppa's playgroup teacher. She looks after Peppa and her friends. Madame Gazelle tells the children that George is coming to play. The children are all very excited about meeting Peppa's little brother.

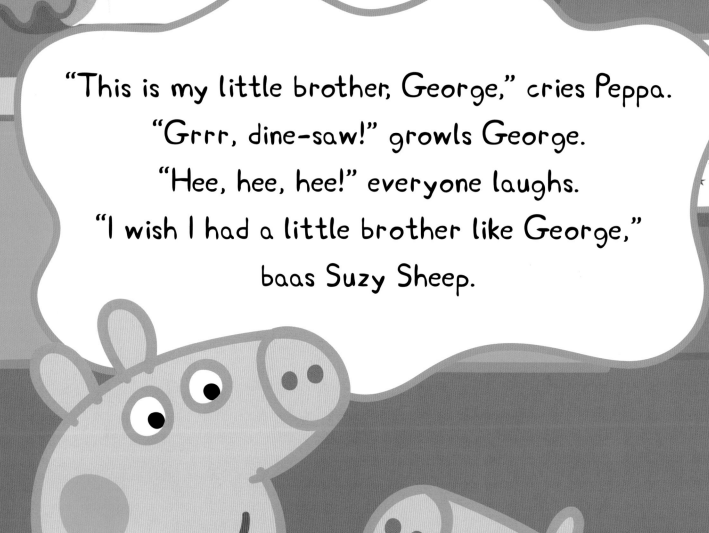

"This is my little brother, George," cries Peppa.
"Grrr, dine-saw!" growls George.
"Hee, hee, hee!" everyone laughs.
"I wish I had a little brother like George,"
baas Suzy Sheep.

George shakes his toy, Mr Dinosaur, at Madame Gazelle, "Grrr! Dine-saw!" "Aah! Really scary!" laughs Madame Gazelle. Peppa is proud of George making everyone laugh. "George is my little brother. He's brilliant," she says.

"Shall we show George how we paint pictures?" Madame Gazelle asks the children.

"George is not very good at painting," says Peppa. "But I can show him how to paint a flower."

"Watch me, George," snorts Peppa.
"First, you paint a big circle."

Peppa carefully dips her brush into a pot of
pink paint and draws a big pink circle
right in the middle of her paper.

George draws a big green circle.
"No, George. That's the wrong colour,"
snorts Peppa. "Watch me."
Peppa makes yellow petal shapes.
George paints a green zigzag.
"George! That's the wrong shape," says Peppa.

Peppa admires her flower painting.
"Perfect," she says, happily.
George is still painting. Instead of a stalk
and leaves he has painted another circle
with five lines sticking out from it.
"You are doing it all wrong!" says Peppa.

"I've painted a flower," says Peppa.
"Very good, Peppa," smiles Madame Gazelle.
"And look, George has painted a dinosaur."
Madame Gazelle sticks Peppa and George's
pictures on the wall.

Now it is time to go home.
"What will you paint next time,
George?" asks Madame Gazelle.
"Dine-saw! Grrr!" giggles George.
"Hee, hee, hee!" everyone laughs.

Dentist Trip

Every morning, Peppa and
George brush their teeth.
Scrub! Scrub! Scrub!

Scrub! Scrub! Scrub!

51

"George, are your teeth
as clean as mine?"
Peppa asks, showing off
her clean white teeth.

"You both have lovely clean teeth.
I'm sure the dentist will be happy!"
calls out Daddy Pig.

Later that day, Peppa and George are at the dentist's, waiting for their check-up. It is George's first visit.

"Peppa! George! The dentist will see you now!" says Miss Rabbit, the nurse. "Hooray!" they both cheer.

This is Doctor Elephant, the dentist.
"Who's first?" he asks.

"I'm first," replies Peppa. "I'm a big girl.
Watch me, George!"

"Open wide, please!" orders
Doctor Elephant, softly.
"Aaaaah . . ." Peppa opens her mouth
as wide as she possibly can.
"Let's take a look!" says the dentist,
checking Peppa's teeth with a mirror.

"There. All done! What lovely
clean teeth!" cheers Doctor Elephant.
"Now you can have the special drink."
Gargle! Ptooou! Peppa spits the
pink liquid out into the sink.
It's George's turn next.

George does not want it to be his turn.
So the dentist lets him hold Mr Dinosaur.
"All done. You have very strong, clean
teeth, George!" smiles Doctor Elephant.

"But wait, what is this?" cries Doctor Elephant. "George has clean teeth, but this young dinosaur's teeth are very dirty."

"The water jet, please, Miss Rabbit!" orders the dentist.
He uses the water to clean Mr Dinosaur's teeth.

Slosh!
Slosh!

Slosh!

"Pink!" cries George, picking up a glass. "That's right, George!" says the dentist. "Mr Dinosaur needs some special pink drink!" Gurgle! Gurgle!

"Gosh! What shiny teeth you have,
Mr Dinosaur!" cries Miss Rabbit.
"Dine-saw! Grrr!" snorts George.

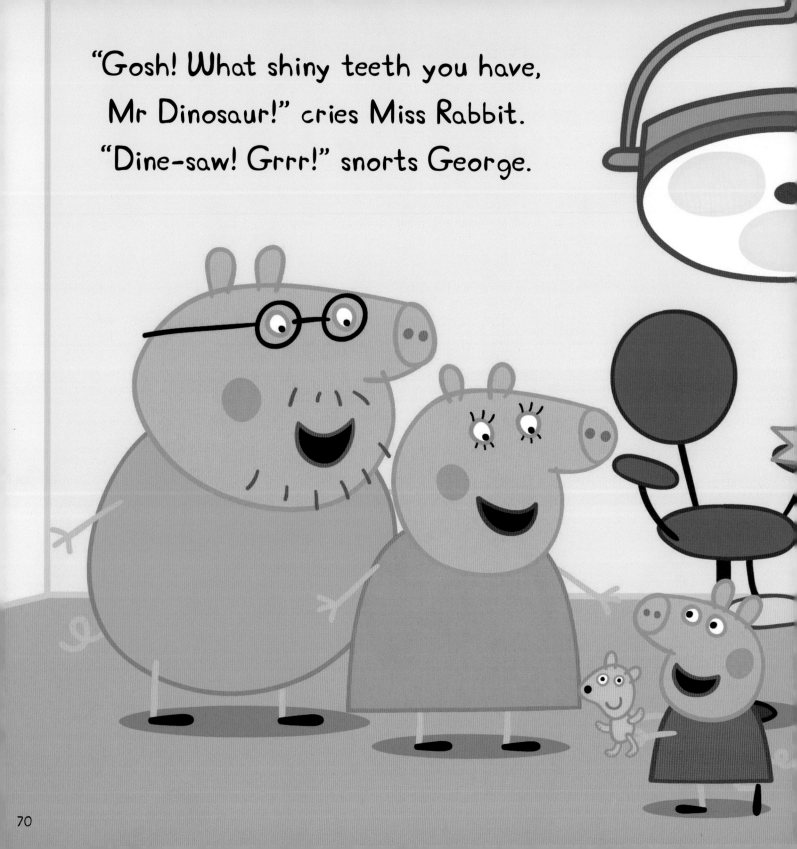

George loves Mr Dinosaur.
Especially now that he has
nice clean teeth.

Nature Trail

Peppa and her family are going on a
nature trail. Mummy Pig asks
Daddy Pig not to forget the picnic.
"As if I would," laughs Daddy Pig.

They head off along the trail with their map.
Oh dear! Daddy Pig has left the picnic in the car.

Mummy and Daddy Pig ask Peppa if she can
see anything interesting in the forest.
"I don't see anything but boring trees," says Peppa.
Then she looks really hard and
finds some footprints on the ground.

"Let's follow the footprints and see who
made them," says Mummy Pig.

"We will have to be very quiet so we don't
scare anything away. Shhhh!"

Peppa and George follow the footprints along the ground.
"It looks like they were made by a little bird," says Mummy Pig.

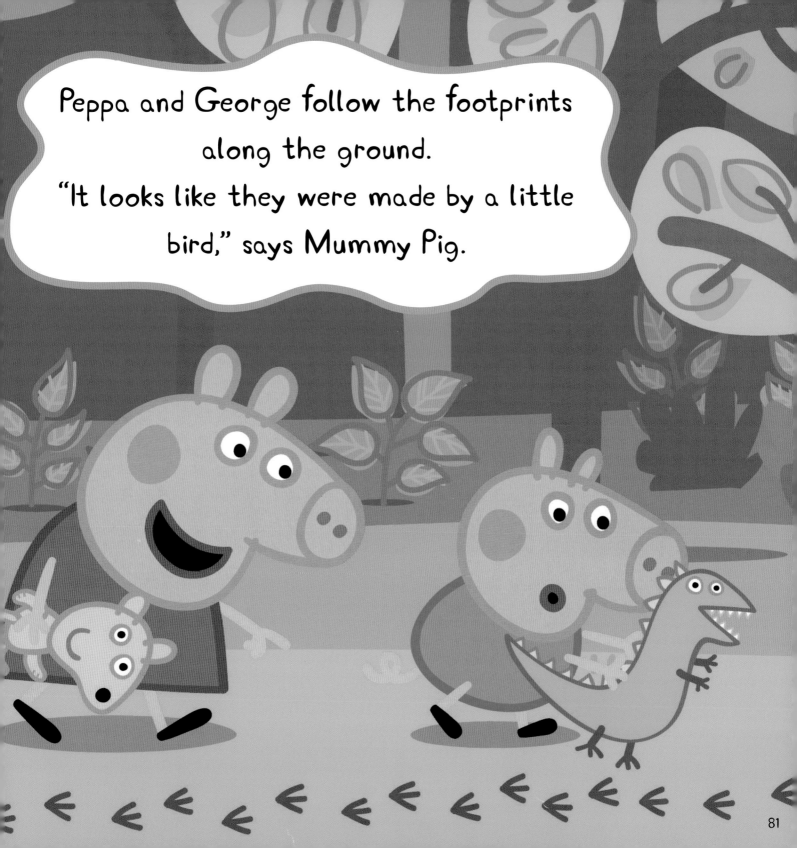

Soon, they come to the
end of the footprints.
"The bird has flown up into
that tree," smiles Daddy Pig.

"Where?" asks Peppa.
Daddy Pig gives Peppa binoculars
to help her see the bird.

George finds some more footprints.
They are very little. Daddy Pig says they
belong to ants collecting leaves to eat.

Munch!

Munch!

"I think it's time for lunch," says Mummy Pig. But Daddy Pig has left the picnic in the car!

"My map is wrong," begins Daddy Pig. "We'll have to follow our own footprints back to the car."

Suddenly, it starts to rain. It washes everyone's footprints away!
"How are we going to find the car, now?" asks Mummy Pig.

Quack!

Quack!

"Ducks love picnics," says Peppa. "Mrs Duck, can you help us find our picnic please?"

The ducks lead Peppa and her
family back to their car.

"We're here! Thank you for your
help, Mrs Duck," cries Peppa.

"I love picnics!" laughs Daddy Pig.
The ducks love picnics too.
Quack! Quack! So do the birds!

And so do the ants!

Munch! Munch!

"Everybody loves picnics!" cries Peppa.

Peppa's First Sleepover

Peppa is going to her very first sleepover at Zoe
Zebra's house. "Welcome to my sleepover!" Zoe says.

"I'll pick you up in the morning," Mummy Pig
says to Peppa with a kiss.

Rebecca Rabbit, Suzy Sheep and
Emily Elephant are already here.
"I've got my teddy," Peppa says.

Zoe has her monkey. Rebecca has her carrot.
Suzy has her owl. And Emily has her frog.

"Don't stay up too late, girls! And don't be too loud.
Daddy Zebra has to get up early to deliver the post,"
Mummy Zebra says as she turns out the lights.

Zoe's baby twin sisters, Zuzu and Zaza,
want to join the sleepover too.
"Sleepovers are only for big girls!" Zoe says.

The twins begin to cry.
"They're so sweet and little," Peppa says.

"Can they stay?" Rebecca asks.
"OK," Zoe says to the twins.
"But you must NOT fall asleep."

"What should we do first?"
Suzy asks.
"I'm having piano lessons!
Listen . . ." Zoe starts to pound
on the keys. "Twinkle, twinkle,
little star . . ."

Mummy Zebra has woken up,
"Shush! You must be quiet so Daddy Zebra can sleep!
Now, into your sleeping bags, please."

"Snort! What do we do now?" Peppa asks.
"At sleepovers, there's always
a midnight feast!" Zoe says.
"It's when we eat things," Suzy says
in a hushed voice. "In secret."

"Shhh!" Zoe says as she leads the girls to the kitchen.
They each grab some delicious fruit, perfect for
a midnight feast. The floorboard creaks.

Oh no! Mummy Zebra has woken up. "You'll wake Daddy Zebra! Now, who knows a bedtime story?"

The girls take turns: "Once upon a time, there was a little fairy . . ." Suzy begins.

"And she lived in the forest . . ." Peppa continues.
"And the fairy met a big monster, who went . . .
RAARRR!" Emily says with a big
elephant trumpet noise!

Oh dear. The noise has woken Daddy Zebra!
"Sorry, Daddy," Zoe says. "There was a story
about a fairy and a scary monster."

"And we want to know what happens next!"
Peppa says. "Very well," Daddy Zebra sighs.
"The monster lifted up his great,
big hairy paws . . ."

"And walked along on his great, big hairy feet . . . And sang . . . 'Twinkle, twinkle, little star, how I wonder what you are . . .'" Daddy Zebra sings gently as he plays the piano.

Daddy Zebra's song has sent everyone to sleep.

Peppa Pig's Family Computer

Mummy Pig is working on the family computer. She is typing very fast. Mummy Pig has a lot of important work to do today.

Daddy Pig is in the kitchen
making soup for lunch.

"Daddy?" Peppa asks. "Can we go and watch
Mummy on the computer, please?"
"Yes, as long as you don't disturb her," Daddy Pig says.

"Mummy?" Peppa asks. "Can George and I sit on your lap and watch you work?"

'Yes, as long as you both sit quietly," Mummy Pig agrees.

About a minute later, Peppa asks, "Can we play the Happy Mrs Chicken game on the computer?"

Mummy Pig says, "We can play Happy Mrs Chicken later. But now I have to work."

Another minute later, Peppa asks, "Mummy? Can we help you work?" Peppa taps away at the computer like Mummy Pig.

"No, Peppa!" Mummy says. "You mustn't touch the computer while I'm working."

131

"Yes, George," Peppa says in a bossy voice.
"You mustn't do this." Peppa taps away again
and the computer flashes.

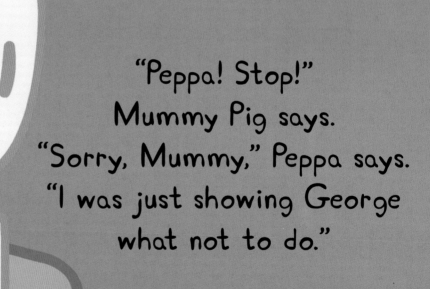

"Peppa! Stop!"
Mummy Pig says.
"Sorry, Mummy," Peppa says.
"I was just showing George
what not to do."

"Daddy Pig!" Mummy calls. "Can you mend the computer while I finish the lunch?"
"Uh . . ." Daddy Pig says. "I'm not very good with these things."

"Hmmm . . ." Daddy Pig pushes a button.

"Mmmm . . ." Daddy Pig pushes another button.

"Maybe if I switch it off and switch it on again . . ."

Daddy Pig has mended the computer!
"Hooray, Daddy!" shouts Peppa.

She and George jump up and down.
"Yes," Daddy Pig smiles. "I am a bit of
an expert at these things."

"Daddy," Peppa asks. "Can we play that computer game, Happy Mrs Chicken? Mummy said we could play it later," Peppa says. "And now it's later!"

"Well," Daddy Pig thinks for a moment,
"OK then." Daddy Pig starts
the Happy Mrs Chicken game.

"Ho, ho, ho!" Daddy Pig laughs as Peppa
and George play Happy Mrs Chicken.
"Snort!" Mummy Pig says as she comes into the room.
"I see the computer is working again!"